MEET THE CREW

WRITTEN BY ELLA PATRICK
ART BY DIOGO SAITO **AND** LUIGI AIMÉ

LOS ANGEL

© & TM 2018 Lucasfilm Ltd.

All rights reserved. Published by Disney • Lucasfilm Press, an imprint
of Disney Book Group. No part of this book may be reproduced or
transmitted in any form or by any means, electronic or mechanical,
including photocopying, recording, or by any information storage and
retrieval system, without written permission from the publisher. For
information address Disney • Lucasfilm Press, 1200 Grand Central
Avenue, Glendale, California 91201.

Printed in the United States of America

First Edition, May 2018   10 9 8 7 6 5 4 3 2 1

Library of Congress Control Number on file

FAC-029261-18109

ISBN 978-1-368-01628-5

Visit the official *Star Wars* website at: www.starwars.com.

SUSTAINABLE
FORESTRY
INITIATIVE

Certified Sourcing

www.sfiprogram.org
SFI-01415

Han and Qi'ra lived on Corellia.

But Corellia was a bad place.

Han and Qi'ra wanted to leave Corellia.

Corellia was full of mean aliens.

Mean aliens like Moloch

and his scary hounds.

And a giant worm named Proxima.

Han and Qi'ra worked for Proxima.

Moloch and Proxima would not let
Han and Qi'ra leave Corellia.

Han and Qi'ra tried to escape.

But Moloch chased them!

Han got away.

Qi'ra did not.

Han joined the Empire
to get off of Corellia.
But he was sent to a muddy planet
called Mimban.

The Empire was fighting
a war on Mimban.

Han did not want to fight in the war.

Han met some people on Mimban
who could help him.
Beckett was gruff.

Val was tough.
And Rio was a pilot
with four arms.

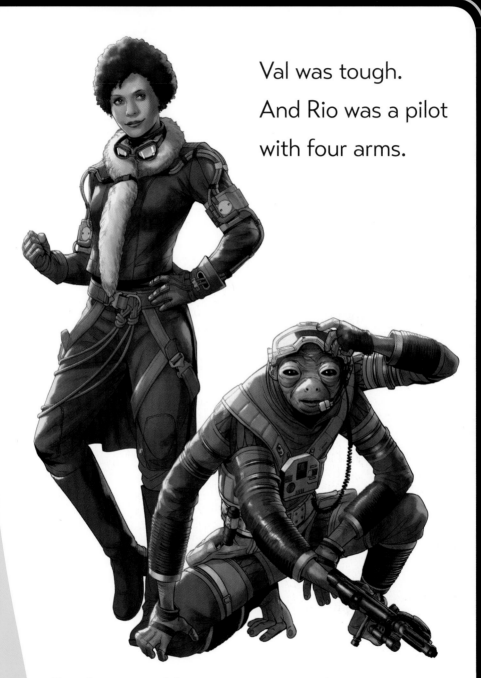

Beckett and his team were there
to steal a ship called an AT-hauler.

Beckett, Val, and Rio helped Han during the battle on Mimban.

Han wanted to leave

Mimban with them.

But stormtroopers captured Han.

The troopers threw Han in a pit
with a muddy Wookiee.

The Wookiee was named Chewbacca.

Han was supposed to fight Chewbacca.

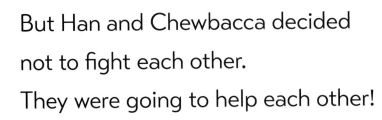

But Han and Chewbacca decided
not to fight each other.
They were going to help each other!
Chewie pushed Han into a beam.

The beam broke,
and the pit caved in.
Han and Chewie escaped!

Han and Chewie chased
Beckett's ship.

They left the Empire and
the muddy planet behind!

Han, Chewie, and Beckett's team
flew to a planet called Vandor.
Beckett needed Han and Chewie
to help him rob an Imperial train.

But Beckett's plan did not work.

Beckett, Han, and Chewie

were in trouble.

They owed a lot of money to a mean man named Dryden Vos.

Dryden Vos had hired Beckett
to rob the train.
Dryden worked for an evil gang
called Crimson Dawn.
Beckett needed to pay Dryden back.

Dryden sent a woman
with Beckett, Han, and Chewie.
It was Han's friend Qi'ra!
Qi'ra would make sure that Beckett,
Han, and Chewie paid Dryden back.

Qi'ra knew someone who
could help them.
His name was Lando.

Lando was nice but tricky.

He liked to play cards.

Lando agreed to help.

Lando had a droid named L3-37.

L3 was smart and loyal.

Lando and L3 had a ship
called the *Millennium Falcon*.

The *Millennium Falcon* was the fastest
ship in the galaxy.

Han had a new crew.
Together, they would
finish the adventure they
had started!